This book belongs to

_____

Excuse me, I'm trying to read!

written by
Mary Jo Amani

illustrated by
Lehla Eldridge

Established in 1921, the National Association of Elementary School Principals (NAESP)
leads in the advocacy and support for elementary- and middle-level principals in the United States, Canada and overseas.
The NAESP Foundation, founded in 1982, is the charitable arm of NAESP and is dedicated to securing and
stewarding private gifts and grants that benefit NAESP.

Excuse Me, I'm Trying to Read
Text Copyright © 2012 by Mary Jo Amani
Illustration Copyright © 2012 by Lehla Eldridge

A Mackinac Island Book
Published by Charlesbridge
85 Main Street
Watertown, MA 02472
(617) 926-0329

www.charlesbridge.com

Library of Congress Cataloging-in-Publication Data on file

Fiction
ISBN 978-1 934133-51-4 (hardcover)
ISBN 978-1 934133-52-1 (paperback)
ISBN 978-1-60734-464-3 (ebook)

Summary: A young girl is repeatedly interrupted by wild animals while trying to read and in turn,
the animals join her for reading adventures of their own.

Packaged by Blue Tree Creative, LLC.
www.bluetreecreative.com

Printed February 2013 by Imago in Singapore.

(hc) 10 9 8 7 6 5 4 3 2
(sc) 10 9 8 7 6 5 4 3

Mackinac Island Press
for the love of reading

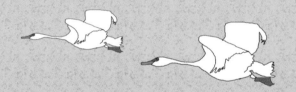

Trying to read with an
elephant can be surprising.

Trying to read with a Marabou stork can be painful.

Excuse me, I'm trying to read!
Will you please take your
sharp claws out
of my hair?

Trying to read with a
snake can be scary.

out of the tree...

ee heee

HA HAHAHAHAH

whawhawhaw
AHAHAHA

Excuse me, I'm trying to read! Will you please stop laughing so loud?

Trying to read with a dung
beetle can be stinky.

Excuse me, I'm trying to read!
Would you please use your little feet to
roll the dung in the other direction?

Trying to read with a crocodile
can be dangerous.

Excuse me, I'm trying to read!
Would you please keep your mouth open?

Trying to read with
an impala can be tricky.

Excuse me, I'm trying to read!
Would you please give me some room?

Trying to read with a
rhinoceros can be risky.

Excuse me, I'm trying to read!
Would you please stop for a moment
so I can take my book off your horn?

Trying to read with a
monkey can be annoying.

Excuse me, I'm trying to read!
Will you please give me my book back?

Trying to read with a lion
can make you sleepy.

Excuse me, I'm trying to read!
Would you please stop purring and
take your paw off my head?

EXCUSE ME...

Special thanks to Olive, Amari, and Jahli Eldridge-Rogers

for their insightful critique that made

all the difference in the world;

to our wonderful husbands, Anthony and Todd,

who have provided feedback and support in

every part of our lives; and to the women

and children of Nwadjahane,

Mozambique who inspired this collaboration.